RACING ACE

Drive It! Fix It!

Written by
Larry Dane Brimner

Illustrated by
Kaylani Juanita

ACORN
SCHOLASTIC INC.

For Sloan Stevens, the original Ace. —LDB

To everyone who trusts me behind the wheel,
I drive slow because you are precious cargo. —KJ

Library of Congress Cataloging-in-Publication Data
Names: Brimner, Larry Dane, author. | Juanita, Kaylani, illustrator.
Title: Drive it! Fix it! / written by Larry Dane Brimner; illustrated by Kaylani Juanita.
Description: New York : Acorn/Scholastic Inc., 2022. | Series: Racing Ace; 1 | Summary: Ace has built her own car, but when she is ready for a test run it will not start, and she has to figure out what part is missing—and then in the middle of the race something else goes wrong.
Identifiers: LCCN 2019044135 | ISBN 9781338553789 (paperback) | ISBN 9781338553796 (library binding)
Subjects: LCSH: Karting—Juvenile fiction. | Racing—Juvenile fiction. | CYAC: Karting—Fiction. | Racing—Fiction.
Classification: LCC PZ7.B767 Dr 2021 | DDC (E)—dc23
LC record available at https://lccn.loc.gov/2019044135

10 9 8 7 6 5 4 3 2   22 23 24 25 26

Printed in the U.S.A.   40

First edition, March 2022
Edited by Katie Carella
Book design by Maria Mercado

READY TO RACE

This is Ace.
She likes to race.

This is Ace's car.

Ace made it herself.

She bolted the parts together.

Then she painted some stripes.

Ace gets her car ready for the race.

She oils the wheels.

She shines each door.

She kicks each tire.

Ace gets ready for the race, too.

She zips up her racing jacket.

She puts on her racing goggles.

She snaps on her helmet.

Ace is almost ready for the big race.
She must try out the track first.

Oh no! The car will not start.
What is wrong?

Ace tightens the bolts.

She pumps air into the tires.

The car still will not start.

Aha! The car needs a part.

No, not that part.

No, not that part.

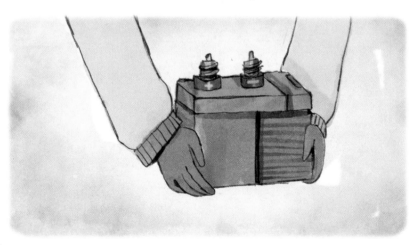

No, no, no, no.

Yes, that is the part to make the car start.

Ace adds the part.

She turns the crank to start the motor.

Now the car is ready, but Ace is not.
What is she missing?

Her racing jacket is zipped.
Her goggles are clean.

Her helmet is
in place.

Aha! Ace remembers what she forgot.

She cannot race without her lucky scarf.

Now Ace is ready. Let's race.

TROUBLE AHEAD

The racers are ready. They are set.
The starter waves the flag. Go!

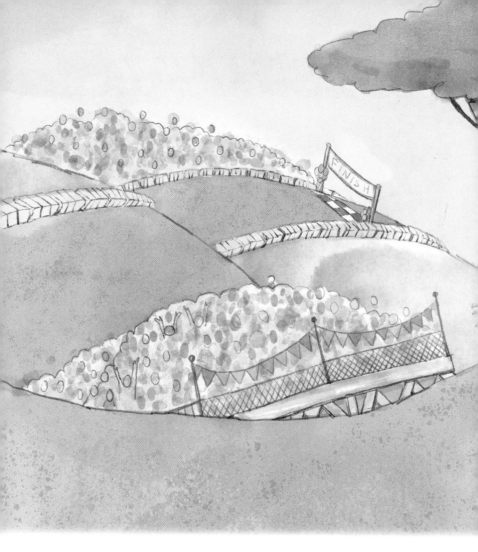

The crowd roars.
Ace and her car go fast at the start.

Two other cars go just as fast.
Yikes, Ace. Go faster!

Three more cars are close behind.
They are getting closer.

Now there are five cars near Ace.
Can she leave them in her dust?

Faster, Ace! Go faster.
Ace tucks her head low.

Faster, Ace! Go even faster.
Ace and her car go far.

Oh no!
Ace's car starts to wobble.

Now her car starts to go slower,

and slower,   and slower.

Two cars zoom past Ace on one side.

ZIP!

ZIP!

ZIP!

Three more fly by on her other side.

Ace is in last place.
Does her car need a new part?

Ace looks to one side.

Then she looks to the other side.

Her car does not need a new part.
The wheels are in a rut!

She bumps her car out of the rut.

Ace is back in the race!

She grips the steering wheel.

She tucks her head.

Ace takes a deep breath.
Can she win the race?

THE FINISH

Ace races downhill.
The finish line is ahead.

Now her car starts to go faster,

and faster,

and faster.

Look at Ace go, go, go!
Now two cars speed down the track.

Ace grits her teeth.
The cars are so close.

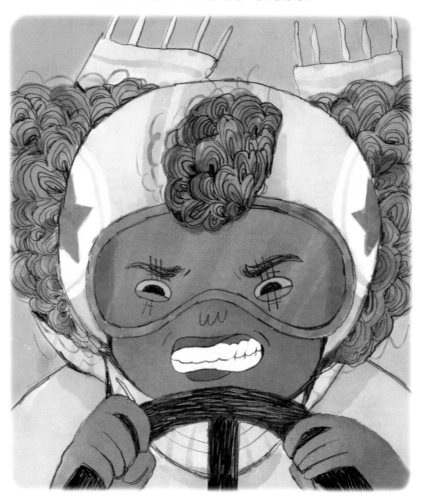

Ace's car inches ahead.

Oh no! It falls behind.

Come on, Ace. Win the race!
You are ready.

There are no more hills to climb.
There are no more racers to pass.

Just the final stretch to race.
Ace crosses the finish line.

The crowd roars.
Ace wins the race.

ABOUT THE CREATORS

LARRY DANE BRIMNER

always wanted a snazzy car like Ace's, but he never got one. Instead, he had a bicycle that he liked to ride fast, faster, fastest . . . until one day he hit a pothole in the road and flew over the handlebars. Now he rides his bicycle in Tucson, Arizona, very slowly.

KAYLANI JUANITA

failed her first driving test because she couldn't remember how to start the car. After plenty of practice, she aced her driving test in Fairfield, California. Now she knows how to start a car, drive it, and park it!

YOU CAN DRAW ACE!

1 Draw Ace's body.

2 Add face details.

3 Draw Ace's racing outfit.

4 Add her helmet and goggles.

5 Add her hair.

6 Color in your drawing!

WHAT'S YOUR STORY?

Ace makes a car for the big race.
Imagine **you** make a car and join the race.
Would your car go faster than Ace's car?
Who would win the race?
Write and draw your story!